GW00857884

FRIENDS NEXT

Three stories about Lucy B....gs, her family and friends, and her life in Codling Village.

Susan Hill is one of Britain's leading writers for both adults and children. Her books for children include another title about Lucy Billing and friends, *A Very Special Birthday*, as well as *Can It Be True?* (winner of the 6–8 years category of the Smarties Book Prize), *Septimus Honeydew*, *Beware, Beware, King of Kings*, *The Christmas Collection* and *The Walker Book of Ghost Stories*. She lives in the Cotswolds, Gloucestershire with her husband and two daughters.

Paul Howard has illustrated a number of stories for Walker, including *Jim's Winter*, *Taking the Cat's Way Home*, *One for Me, One for You*, *Care of Henry* and the picture books *John Joe and the Big Hen*, *Rosie's Fishing Trip* and *A Year in the City*. He is married and lives in London.

After that, they did each other's hair.

STORIES FROM CODLING VILLAGE

FRIENDS
NEXT DOOR

Written by
SUSAN HILL

Illustrations by
PAUL HOWARD

WALKER BOOKS
AND SUBSIDIARIES

LONDON • BOSTON • SYDNEY

First published in Great Britain 1990 by
Julia MacRae Books
This edition published 1992 by Walker Books Ltd
87 Vauxhall Walk
London SE11 5HJ

4 6 8 10 9 7 5

This book is typeset in Plantin.

Printed in England

British Library Cataloguing in Publication Data
A catalogue record for this book
is available from the British Library.

ISBN 0-7445-2426-1

CONTENTS

*One morning, Lucy Billings opened the door
of Beehive Cottage.*

FRIENDS NEXT DOOR

One morning, Lucy Billings opened the door of the cottage where she lived, which was called Beehive Cottage, and went outside. She walked past her brother Ben's bicycle, around the corner and down the path to the gate. Just beside the gate was a wooden box set into the wall, and by standing on the old stepping stone beside it, Lucy could reach up and take out the letters and newspapers that had been left there. (Frank, the milkman, put the milk for Beehive Cottage in the box too, but there were always five bottles, which Lucy couldn't manage safely, so her father or mother or Ben had to collect those.)

This morning, her father had taken the paper to work with him, but there were four letters and a small parcel and Lucy had just reached in and taken them out and closed the door of the box when she saw a blue car come slowly down the lane past Beehive Cottage, and stop by the gate of the house next door. There were two people in the front of the car, a man and a lady, and two children, a girl and a baby, in the back. And when the car stopped, the man got out and pushed open the big wooden gate of the house next door and wedged it with a stone, and then he got back into the car again and they all drove into the drive. For a moment, Lucy stared and stared after them. Then she scrambled down from the stepping stone and ran indoors, holding tightly onto the letters.

"Some people have come!" she said, and

she almost tripped over the doorstep, she was so excited, "some people in a blue car have come to the house next door."

"What sort of car?" asked her brother Ben. He was cutting out a model from the back of the cornflakes box.

"I don't know what sort of a car. A blue car."

"What sort of people then?" asked Ben.

"A man and a lady and a little girl like me and a baby like Rosie."

"And a boy?"

"No," said Lucy, "no boy."

Ben made a face and went back to his cutting.

Then Lucy very much wanted to go back outside and see what was happening, because she thought that the people in the car had looked very interesting people indeed, so she hopped up and down on one foot until her mother said she might go, provided she put on her wellington boots, and Lucy didn't mind doing that in the least because they were brand new boots, red ones, and she was very pleased with them.

"Don't go out of the gate, mind," her mother said, and Lucy said no, she wouldn't because she never did, and Rosie the baby banged her spoon very loudly on the tray of her high chair and laughed and laughed for no reason in particular, the way she often did.

Then Lucy ran all the way down nearly to the very bottom of the garden, to where there was an open bit of fence, and climbed carefully up.

The house next door was called Old Leas Farm. A very long time ago, long, long before Lucy was born, there had been pigs

Lucy climbed carefully up the bit of open fence.

in the pigsties and cows in the dairy and hens in the yard and ducks on the pond and sheep in the fields all around. But they had gone and the farm had been empty and tumbledown and the garden had grown as wild as wild, with grasses as tall as Lucy and nettlebeds everywhere.

Then, just after her birthday, which was in the spring, the workmen had arrived. They were called Bob and Steve and Alf and Gary and George, and they had been very nice, friendly, cheerful, whistly workmen, and Lucy and her brother Ben had often climbed up on the fence and looked over to watch them at work.

They had pulled down and cleared, they had hammered and sawed and drilled; a bulldozer and an earth mover and a cement mixer had arrived, and Ben had spent ages hanging over the fence every afternoon when he got home from school. Sometimes, one of the workmen had come to the back door of Beehive Cottage and asked Mrs Billings to fill their flask with hot water for tea, and Rosie the baby had sat in her pram and waved her arms at them or banged her spoon on the high chair tray and laughed and laughed and made them laugh back. She had laughed at Bob the most because he always wore a blue woolly hat with a red bobble on the top and the bobble had bobbled about when he wagged his head, which he did every time he came, just to make Rosie laugh. But Lucy had liked Steve best because he called her funny names – nice-funny ones, like "Princess" and "Sunbeam" and "Flower".

Then one day Gary had come for the tea-water and told them he had a new baby at home, and that it was a little girl, and they had all said "Hurrah". And then he had said that he and Mrs Gary had decided they would call the baby Lucy, because he'd heard Lucy Billings' mother calling *her* so often over the fence he thought it was the best name of all for a little girl. Then Lucy Billings and her mother and Ben had said "Hurrah" even louder and Rosie had banged and banged her spoon until the tray of the high chair rang and they had all put their hands over their ears.

But one day, Bob and Steve and Alf and Gary and George had finished working on Old Leas Farmhouse and come to Beehive Cottage to say goodbye. Bob had given Mrs Billings a box of chocolates, to say thank you for all the tea-water she had boiled for them, and there were packets of fruity sweets for Ben and Lucy and some jellies for baby Rosie, and they had all gone to the gate to wave goodbye and Lucy had felt very sad, seeing their cars and vans drive away for the last time.

After that, the house next door had been empty and quiet all over again. Until today.

If she stood on tiptoe on the very top of the open bit of fence, Lucy could just see the back of the blue car, which was parked where the old pigsties used to be. But for quite a long time there wasn't anything else to see, and it was just beginning to drizzle a little bit of soft, drizzly rain onto her hands and her head, and she was thinking that she might as well go back inside, when out of the back door of Old Leas Farm came the little girl. She had plaits and a red coat and when she saw Lucy standing on the fence and looking at her she stopped, and looked back, and they both looked, and went on looking for quite a long time, until Lucy thought that any moment they might be finished with looking and say something. But just as she felt that she was ready to, somebody called, "Jane! Jane!" and the girl turned and ran back. Only just as she went into the door again, she looked over her shoulder and Lucy thought that she smiled. So she smiled back. But then the girl was gone.

Lucy waited and waited and jigged about on the fence, but the other girl did not come out again and after a bit it began to rain hard and Lucy's mother shouted to her to hurry in. So she took one last look at the blue car and the empty yard and the tidy garden, before climbing carefully down off the fence and running back to Beehive Cottage.

For the next few days, Lucy asked and asked her mother about the people in the blue car. She asked if she thought they had

She looked over her shoulder and Lucy thought she smiled.

bought the house next door and when they might be moving in and what their names could be – apart from the girl's name, which was Jane, she already knew. And Lucy's mother got very tired of saying, "I really don't know, Lucy," and, "You'll just have to wait and see."

Every night when Lucy went upstairs to bed she stood at the window of her room, which was at the very top of Beehive Cottage, and looked over at Old Leas Farmhouse and the empty yard and the tidy garden and the blank, dark windows and wondered and wondered. Some of her wanted it to stay empty and dark forever because that's how it had been ever since she could remember. Once, she had heard a fox bark from the garden there and Father said it had been on the prowl, just in case there might still be hens left, even after all these years. "Ghosty hens," her brother Ben had said and made Whooooo-whoooooo noises and flapped his arms, until their mother had told him to stop being silly.

When Lucy had gone to bed that night she had looked rather anxiously out of her window and over the wall, in case she might see the ghosty hens, and in the night she had woken up and listened and thought about the empty house and the yard and the garden, rather a lot.

But in the morning, when she looked again, she had seen that it wasn't frightening at all, but just the same, friendly-looking place she had always known, and cheerful, too, in spite of being empty and quiet. Only it seemed a bit lonely. Lucy decided that was what was wrong. And then another part of her very much wanted people to come and live in it and cheer it up and keep it company.

Nothing else happened for over a month, so that Lucy almost forgot about the people in the blue car and stopped asking her mother about them. And then, one Tuesday, something *did* happen, something very surprising and interesting indeed.

Every morning, Lucy went to the Codling Village playgroup. It was held in the village hall, at the other end of Codling Village from Beehive Cottage, and Lucy and her mother, with Rosie in the pushchair, walked there and on the way they collected Sam Smith, who lived at Number 5, Codling, and took him to playgroup, too. Then, at the end of each morning, Sam Smith's mother brought Lucy and Sam back home.

On this particular Tuesday, it was a very

leafy, blowy sort of day, with the wind rushing around and puffing into them, and the leaves swirling down from the trees, and Lucy had run about with Sam trying to catch them. Then they had both gone shuffle-shuffle-shuffle through all the piles of fallen leaves, so that by the time they reached Beehive Cottage, Lucy was feeling quite tired and ready for dinner, too.

Sometimes, Sam Smith and his mother came in to see Lucy's mother, and stayed for a cup of coffee. But today, the Smiths were going to town in Mrs Smith's old car, so they just saw Lucy in through her gate, and watched while she ran up the path and around the corner of the house and turned to wave goodbye to them. The back door of Beehive Cottage was open, and as she went in, she heard her mother say, "Oh good, here's Lucy now."

But then she felt suddenly shy, as well as surprised.

And there in the kitchen, sitting around the big table with her mother, were the lady who had come in the blue car to the house next door, and the girl with plaits called Jane. And sitting on the mat feeding each other with chewed-up crusts of bread were Rosie and another baby girl the same size, with curls like little corkscrews all over her head, and a plump little cheeky face.

Lucy was so astonished that she stood stock-still and her mouth opened into an O. But then she felt suddenly shy, as well as surprised. Her own kitchen seemed to be so full of people she didn't know, and she went around to the other side of the table quickly and pressed very close to her mother and hid her head. Her mother hugged her and laughed and said, "*Now* you can find out what's going to happen in the house next door! You were asking me and asking me, remember? Well, this is Jane Jones, and her mother, and that's Jack Jones, on the floor with Rosie."

"*Jack* Jones?" Lucy said, and pulled away from her mother at once and went to stare at the baby with the corkscrew curls and the plump little cheeky face, and then everyone burst out laughing and Mrs Jones said, "Oh dear, Daddy was right, he *does* look like a little girl, we'll have to get his hair cut." And Jane Jones and Lucy both said exactly at the same moment, "Oh no, you mustn't!" Then they all laughed even more, and the babies on the mat looked up and saw everyone looking at them with laughing faces, so they both laughed too.

Lucy's mother said, "Well, I think that's broken the ice," which Lucy thought was a very odd sort of thing to say on a blowy, leafy, autumn-sunshine sort of day.

24

But then she said, "Do stay and have some lunch with us, won't you? It'll just be some soup and a sandwich," and Mrs Jones said thank you very much, they would like to, if it wasn't too much trouble, and Lucy saw that Jane Jones was looking and looking at her, so she said, "Can you do handstands?"

"No," said Jane Jones.

"Nor can I. Can you do cartwheels?"

"No," said Jane Jones.

"Nor can I. Can you go up very, very high on a swing?"

"*Oh yes!*" said Jane Jones.

"So can I. Let's go and do it."

So Lucy led the way out of the back door and down the garden to the orchardy bit at the bottom, where Mr Billings had fixed swings on to the branches of two old apple trees. They saw that lots of apples had fallen onto the grass in the wind that morning, so

Lucy picked two up and gave one to Jane Jones, and they got onto the two swings. First Lucy swung very, very high, and then Jane Jones swung very, very high, and then they both swung high together, and after that, they just sat holding onto their swings with one hand and munching their apples with the other, and the swings rocked gently to and fro.

"We're coming to live next door," Jane Jones said. "We're moving in next week."

And Lucy looked at her and smiled, and Jane Jones smiled back, and then they swung to and fro again and ate their apples a bit more.

Then Lucy said, "I've never had a friend-next-door before," and Jane Jones said, "Nor have I," and they smiled at each other again. And then, quite suddenly Lucy felt a great rush of happiness bubbling up inside her. She threw away her apple core and stood up on the swing and began to swing very hard and high indeed, and felt herself sailing up almost over the tops of the apple trees and into the sky and the wind blew her hair about and she shouted, "We're friends-next-door." Jane began to swing high standing up, too, and they both shouted, "We're friends-next-door," and laughed and shouted and swung in the wind, with the leaves and the apples falling all around them, until it was time to go in for dinner.

*Lucy Billings heard someone calling and calling
in the garden of the house next door.*

THE STORY OF
QUEENIE AND TREACLE

One fine Saturday morning, Lucy Billings heard someone calling and calling in the garden of the house next door. At first it was just one voice but after a few minutes there were two. So she ran upstairs to her bed-room and looked out of the window, and from there, she could see Jane Jones and her mother going up and down their garden and they were both calling and calling. Only Lucy couldn't hear exactly *what* they were calling and she very much wanted to know. So she ran downstairs again and out of the back door and all the way up to the end of the garden of Beehive Cottage, to where there was an open bit of fence. She climbed up on the fence and looked over the top and then she could see *and* hear. Jane Jones and her mother were looking, under the hedge and beside the hedge and in the sheds, and as they looked they both called, "Queenie! Queenie!" over and over again.

Lucy knew quite well who Queenie was. A week ago, when Jane Jones and her mother and father and brother Jack had moved into the house next door, Queenie had come too, in a wicker basket with a lid. When Lucy had gone round with her mother to take a tray of tea and cakes for them all, because the electricity at Old Leas Farmhouse wasn't working yet, the basket had been in the middle of the kitchen floor, and it had been making a frightful noise, a sort of squealy-mewly-yeowly sort of noise. And when Lucy had bent down and lifted up a corner of the basket, there had been two green eyes and one brown and one black pointed ear, and a pair of white whiskers. Later, when all the doors were closed, Mrs Jones had let them open the lid of the wicker basket right up and there had been Queenie. She was a very pretty, very dainty, very small cat, and she looked as if someone had taken a brush full of brown paint and a brush full of orange paint and a brush full of black, and painted a bit of each here and there, just as the fancy took them, and then added a dab of white for luck.

"Not a proper tortoiseshell cat, I'm afraid," Mrs Jones had said.

"Not a proper anything," Jane Jones had said.

"In fact, a bit of a mess really," Mr Jones had said.

But then they had *all* said that they loved her just the same, and that was why they were being very careful only to let her out of the basket when all the doors were closed. Because Old Leas Farmhouse would be very strange indeed to Queenie, it would look strange and feel strange and most of all, it would smell strange, and she would be very puzzled and very frightened until she got quite used to living there and had learned her way about properly.

"If we open the door now, and Queenie gets out, she'll just try to run back to our old house, and that's such a long way away that she'd be lost almost at once," said Mrs Jones.

So they had stroked and petted Queenie and then let her explore the kitchen. She had got out of the basket and sniffed and looked and sniffed and crept, twitching her whiskers and waving her tail, and occasionally just sitting down and yeowling

*She had got out of the basket and sniffed
and looked and sniffed and crept.*

a great, sad yeowl. After a while, Mrs Jones had put her back in the basket and closed the lid, and the basket had creaked and heaved about for a minute and then gone quite quiet and still.

"She's asleep," said Jane Jones.

So when Lucy stood on the open bit of fence and saw Jane and her mother going up and down, and heard them calling and calling, she guessed at once what had happened.

"Did Queenie get out?" she shouted to them. "Have you lost her?"

And Jane Jones said yes, they had. "And she's been lost since last night and we've called and called her and put out a dish of milk and we can't find her anywhere and perhaps she'll be lost forever and ever," she said, and then she began to cry, so that Lucy thought she must certainly not stand there on the fence but go and help look for Queenie straight away.

"I'm going to ask if I can come," she shouted to Jane Jones and quickly scrambled down from the fence and ran indoors. Her mother had already said that Jane could come and play at Beehive Cottage for the morning if she would like to, and Lucy had thought all over again how very nice it was to have a friend-next-door.

So she rushed into the kitchen and said, "Jane Jones has lost Queenie, they opened the door and she got out and they're calling and calling but they can't find her any- where and please may I go and help them look?"

"Yes, I heard them calling," her mother said. "Oh dear. Wait a minute and I'll come with you. But first we should really see if

35

she's got through the hedge into our garden and is hiding anywhere here."

Then Lucy's mother picked up Rosie the baby out of her playpen, where she had been piling up plastic bricks and knocking them down again, and they all went outside and joined in the search.

They searched under the hedge bottom on their side all the way around the garden, and inside the tool shed and the wood store and the garage and the loft above the garage. They called and called and called, and in the garden of the house next door, Jane Jones and her mother went on searching and calling. And in the middle of it all, Lucy heard the whiny noise of Frank's milk float, so she ran down the drive to the front gate, where Frank was just taking out the five bottles of milk to put in their box.

"Hello, jam-pot, how are you today?"

Frank the milkman always had a different name for Lucy, and a lot of names were very silly; they were names like "lettuce leaf" and "teacup" and "cough drop", and they made Lucy laugh. But today she didn't laugh, she said at once, "Jane Jones has lost her cat Queenie, they left a door open and she got out and they've searched and searched and called and called and so have we but we can't find her anywhere."

And Frank said, "Dear me, I don't like to hear that. You tell me what this little Queenie-cat looks like, and I'll keep my eye open. She won't have gone far."

"She's brown and orange and black, all mixed up with some white bits, and Mrs Jones says she might try to go back to where they lived before and that's a very long way away."

"No, no, she'll be used to the new smells

Frank banged the gate shut.

by now, and she'll know this is where she lives because her people are here, you see, and all the chairs and tables and rugs as well." And Frank banged the gate shut and climbed back into his milk float with a cheerful smile.

"I'll keep an eye open. We'll find little Queenie-cat, she won't be far away." And he winked at Lucy and off went the milk float, whiny-whiny-rattle-chink up the lane.

But Lucy wasn't sure, and a bit later, when Jane Jones and her mother came into Beehive Cottage, *they* weren't sure either, and Jane said she thought Queenie was lost forever, and began to cry again.

"Come upstairs and play, and I'll let you dress and undress Violet, if you like," said Lucy. Violet was her last-birthday doll, and still very special. So she and Jane Jones went upstairs and played with Violet, and after that, they did each other's hair and used Lucy's mother's slides and grips and hair combs to make themselves into grown-up ladies, and they almost – but not quite – forgot about Queenie, and Jane didn't cry any more. Only once she said, in the middle of pulling off Violet's petticoat, "But she wouldn't have come to your house because of Jessie. She's frightened of dogs." Jessie was the Billings family's big black labrador.

"Well, Frank the milkman said he'd look out for her, and tell everybody, and he said she wouldn't have got far."

"Oh," said Jane. But she didn't look very happy.

That afternoon, they all went in Mrs Jones's car to the park in Stillford, where there was a playground with slides and swings and a rope-walk and a roundabout, and a pond with ducks. Afterwards, they walked under the chestnut trees collecting conkers in two carrier bags. Rosie and Jack got out of their pushchairs and ran about and tried to find conkers too, but usually they brought back handfuls of leaves and a few stones instead. The sun was shining and they all got quite warm and piled their coats into the push-chairs and then ran about a lot more, before going to the café in the park, where they sat at tables outside on the grass. They had orange squash and scones and jam and chocolate biscuits, and it was only when she was finishing her second biscuit that Jane Jones suddenly said, "But if she's lost forever, who will give Queenie anything to eat?" and burst out crying all over again. Her mother hugged her and said of course they would find Queenie in the end, they'd go home now, at once, and carry on searching.

"And Daddy will look."

"And *my* daddy will," said Lucy.

"Yes," said Jane, "and all the daddies in Codling Village."

And so they did. Or at least, a great many of them, and a lot of other people besides, because Frank the milkman had been around and asked them to. And Jane Jones' mother wrote out two notices on postcards. They read:

> LOST
> QUEENIE, our small brown,
> orange and black cat with
> white whiskers. If found,
> please return to
> OLD LEAS FARMHOUSE.

Then they walked up to Mrs Dobby's post office shop, and she kindly said she would put one of the notices in her window, and they pinned the other one on the village notice board by the telephone box. "There," said Mrs Jones, "now Queenie is sure to be found."

But she wasn't. Not that day or the next or the next, even though Lucy's father and Jane Jones' father went all the way down Magpie Lane to the fields and even as far as the wood, searching in the hedges and ditches with sticks, and Mr Day at Codling Farm let them go into his barns and hayrick and stables and cowsheds and outhouses to look, too. They said they had seen just about every other kind of cat there, because Mr Day had so many farm cats he'd lost count. But not Queenie.

On the fourth day, which was Wednesday, the most astonishing thing happened. Lucy and Jane Jones had come back from the

"What has she got?" Jane Jones shouted,
"Oh, whatever has Queenie got?"

playgroup, and they were playing in the outside yard of Old Leas Farmhouse with a lot of cardboard boxes and packing cases which had been used to bring all the Jones' things when they had moved, and which Mr Jones hadn't got round to breaking up or burning yet. They hoped very much that he wouldn't, because the boxes made excellent houses and railway carriages and tea tables. And in the middle of playing, Jane Jones happened to look round, and said, "Oh look, oh look! It's Queenie. Queenie's come home!"

Lucy looked, and there, walking daintily down the garden, came the little brown and orange and black cat, Queenie. And she was carrying something very carefully in her mouth.

"What has she got?" Jane Jones shouted, "Oh, whatever has Queenie got?"

Just then, Mrs Jones came out of the back door holding Jack, and they all looked as Queenie walked towards them. She came right up to where they stood and then she stopped in front of Jane.

"It's a kitten!" Jane Jones said.

And so it was. A small, browny-yellowy coloured kitten. Queenie set it down very gently on the cobbles and gave a loud meowl, and the kitten looked up at them all and gave a meowl that was almost as loud.

"Is it *her* kitten?" Lucy asked.

"Oh no, it can't be," Mrs Jones said, and she bent down and stroked the kitten's head. "It's quite big – two or three weeks old, anyway, and we've only been here a week and Queenie certainly didn't have a kitten when we came."

"Then whose is it? Where did she get it from?" asked Jane and Lucy together.

But of course Mrs Jones didn't know. Nor did anybody else, though they asked all about Codling Village, and even put up another two notices saying:

FOUND
One browny-yellow kitten.
Please claim from
OLD LEAS FARMHOUSE.

But nobody did claim him and nobody had any idea whose kitten it was either, and where Queenie had gone to for those four days was a mystery, too.

"I told you she wouldn't have gone far away," said Frank the milkman, when he heard. Only Lucy thought that she might have been, she might have been miles and miles and miles. But nobody would ever be able to find out.

*What the kitten liked best was following
Lucy Billings home to Beehive Cottage.*

Mrs Dobby at the post office shop was very glad to hear that Queenie had come home, but she wasn't a bit surprised. "That's cats for you," she said, "they just turn up when they feel like it."

But the oddest thing of all was that although Queenie had brought the kitten back in her mouth, and they seemed to be very happy together, what the kitten liked best was following Lucy Billings home to Beehive Cottage, and sometimes even to come to look for her when she was already there without Jane Jones. However often they took it back to the house next door, sooner or later it would just turn up again, so that in the end, Lucy's father said they might just as well give in and keep it. Only Lucy's mother said she wasn't so sure about that, they had quite enough mouths to feed as it was.

But one cold morning, they came downstairs in to the kitchen to find the kitten curled up with Jessie in her basket by the range, and after that, Lucy's mother said it looked as if the kitten had got its feet under the table. Which Lucy thought was a very odd thing to say.

Then her father asked Lucy what she wanted to call the kitten and said, "I think Turn-up would be about right, myself," but Lucy said you couldn't call a cat Turn-up.

"I shall call it Treacle," she said, "because it looks like that."

After that, Treacle usually slept in Jessie's basket, curled up together with Jessie. Only sometimes, for no particular reason, it went off and lived at the house next door for a day or two. But it always came back, and after a while, Queenie even came with it occasionally and wasn't frightened of Jessie any more, though she would never actually get right into the basket, like Treacle.

"They're a bit like you two, those cats," Jane Jones' mother said, one afternoon to Jane and Lucy, "living in each other's houses half the time!" Which was perfectly true!

A Really Big Shop.

SNOWED IN

One morning in January, when it was still holiday time, so there was no playgroup to go to, Lucy Billings's mother said, "I think we'll go to town today. I want to do a Really Big Shop."

Lucy was very pleased to hear that, because a Really Big Shop meant that they would drive all the way to the big supermarket on the road outside Stillford, and when they were there, Rosie the baby would ride in the shopping trolley, while Lucy helped to fetch things from the shelves and put them in. Then, when Mrs Billings had paid the money and they had loaded their shopping into the car, they would all go back and have a drink and a sticky currant bun in the supermarket café.

So that is what they did. They had so much shopping that Lucy's mother said she wondered if there would be room for them to squeeze back in the car again. They had bought such a great many things because they had run out of nearly everything after Christmas, and because Mrs Billings didn't want to have to come to the big supermarket again for quite a long time, she wanted to make her marmalade instead.

But they all *did* manage to squeeze back into the car, though they were very squashed up next to the cardboard boxes and bags full of cat food and dog food and washing powder and biscuits and flour and sugar and tea and soap and orange juice and cooking oil and baked beans and butter and salt and spaghetti and cheese and vinegar.

Lucy thought that it wasn't really very exciting shopping, not like the shopping they had done before Christmas. But she could see that you couldn't have that all the time, and in a way, she decided that it was nice to be back to the ordinary-everyday.

So she sat in the back of the car next to Rosie the baby, who was strapped into her special seat, and they ate a ginger biscuit each, to help pass the time. Then Lucy played "Round and round the garden, like a teddy bear" on Rosie's hand, and "This little piggy went to market" on her toes (because Rosie the baby always took her shoes and socks off in the car) and Rosie laughed and chuckled and kicked her legs and they had a fine time, until they got far past the town and off the big main road and right out into the country. Then Rosie went fast asleep quite suddenly, and that made

Lucy feel tired, too, and want to be at home by the fire.

Mrs Billings said, "Goodness me, just look at that sky!" Lucy looked out of the car window and saw that they were just climbing the big hill past the wood, so that in a few minutes more they would be in Codling Village. There was always a lot of sky to see here. Lucy thought it was a bit like being under a pudding bowl that someone had turned upside down; and sometimes, when it was windy, she and brother Ben came up here with Mr Billings to fly the red and green kite with the long, long tail.

Only now, Lucy could see that the sky was very, very dark – not dark with the night coming on, but dark with thick dark clouds. So she said, "I think it is going to rain in a minute."

But Mrs Billings said, "I don't think it's

going to rain, *I* think it's going to snow! Those are big fat snow clouds."

"Snow!" Lucy said, and felt very excited, because it was more than a whole year since it had snowed; it was when Rosie the baby had been Rosie the tiny baby, and Lucy and brother Ben had made a snowman in the garden, and a snow house, too, a round one with a little door and a scooped-out inside that they could just crawl into.

"Will it really, truly snow?"

"Yes," said her mother, "I think that it really, truly will!"

And sure enough, by the time they got out of the car at Beehive Cottage the first few flakes of snow were beginning to float down out of the sky.

But it was much too cold to stay looking at them, so they went in quickly and shut the door and Mrs Billings put the kettle on, and Rosie the baby woke up and was cross, so Lucy tried to cheer her up by making funny faces, and Jessie the big black labrador dog came up, all pleased to see them, so that they quite forgot what might be going on outside.

But later, when Mr Billings came home from work, Lucy saw that the sleeves of his coat and the top of his head had snow on them. And when she was going to bed, she looked out of the window of her room at the top of the house, and saw that the window-ledge was white and that the sky was full of pale, swirly flakes of snow. There were so many and they were coming so fast that they muddled up and danced about in front of her. And when she got into bed and had had her story, and her mother had turned the light off, she could still see the white, swirly flakes, even when she shut her eyes tight.

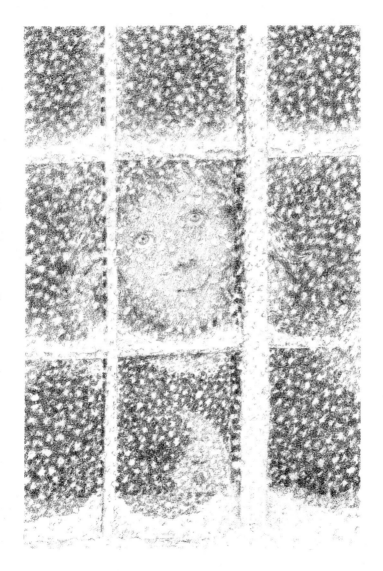

*The window-ledge was white and the sky
was full of pale, swirly flakes of snow.*

Mrs Billings said, "I think it's a very good job indeed that we did our big shop today," and when Lucy asked her why, she said, "Because if it goes on snowing as hard as this all night, I don't think we shall be able to go very far at all in the morning."

"Why? Whatever do you mean?" asked Lucy.

"Because we might be snowed in," her mother said.

"What is 'snowed in'?"

"It means that there might be so much snow that it will all pile up down the lane and up the drive, and especially if it gets windy, and the wind drives the snow in great heaps and drifts to the bottom of our lane. We won't be able to get out of the path at all. It happened once before, when you were very small."

But however much Lucy tried to imagine

just what that would be like, she couldn't, and after a short time, she was so tired that she gave up trying and went to sleep instead.

In the middle of the night she woke up and heard the wind blowing, whoo-whooo-whoo down the chimney and rattling at the window and whistling under the door – because Beehive Cottage was a very, very old cottage and there were lots of cracks and gaps for the wind to blow through. Then Lucy remembered the snow and what her mother had said about if the wind blew all the way down to the bottom of the lane. She wasn't sure whether she was excited or frightened, so she pulled up her covers and slid further down underneath them, where it was warm and dark and cosy, and went back to sleep as quickly as possible.

When she woke up again the next morning, she thought for a moment that it must be summer again, because the sun was shining so very brightly through her curtains-with-the-cherries-on. But when she hopped out of bed and went to the window and opened the curtains, she said a little "Oh!" of surprise. Because the world outside was white. It was the sun, shining out of a blue, blue sky onto the whiteness that had made the light so bright.

There was snow, deep, thick, soft, bright, white snow, everywhere that Lucy Billings could see. Snow in a fat bolster along the window-ledge and snow on the roofs of the shed and the henhouse and all along the fence, and snow on the roof of the house next door, where Jane Jones lived, and snow covering every branch of every tree in the orchardy bit of the garden, just as if Lucy's mother had piped them with icing, like the biscuits she had piped at Christmas.

Then Lucy ran downstairs without even putting on her slippers, and straight into the kitchen, where her mother was just lifting Rosie the baby into her high chair for breakfast, and she said,

"It snowed! It really and truly snowed!"

Just at that moment, Lucy's father opened the back door and banged his boots on the step to knock the snow off them. Then he came inside and said, "Yes, it *has* really and truly snowed and we are really and truly snowed in!"

But then Lucy's mother said to hush because she wanted to listen to what they were saying on the radio, and she turned it up louder, so that they could all hear the radio man telling them about the snow, and which roads were closed and which buses were not running, and then, which villages were quite cut off. And after a minute he said,

"Little Miston" (which was near), "Griffield" (which was much nearer), "Green Hampton" (which was the village right next door). And then he said, "Codling Village."

Lucy jumped up and down and shouted, "Hurrah!" and brother Ben waved both his arms in the air above his head, and Rosie the baby banged and banged her spoon on the tray of her high chair. And Lucy's mother said *wasn't* it a good job she'd done the Really Big Shop the day before, so that now they could all have porridge!

And they did, big bowls of creamy porridge with brown sugar on, and top-of-the-milk too, only they had to be rather careful with that and just have a little splash each, because Lucy's mother said that they couldn't tell when Frank the milkman would be able to get down the lane to them next.

And when they were all full of the hot, comforting porridge, and of toast and honey as well, Lucy's father clapped his hands and said, "Right, gang – work to do!"

So he and Mrs Billings and Lucy and brother Ben all got dressed in their warm outdoor things, and went outside (but Rosie the baby went back to her cot for her morning nap).

There were two big shovels for the grown-ups, and two small spades (which they had used in the sand on their summer holiday) for Lucy and Ben. And then they all began to dig a path through the snow. Only Lucy kept stopping, partly because it was such hard work, but mostly because she kept wanting to look around. She thought that the snow was so beautiful and strange, and that it made her own house and garden, and everywhere else as well, look quite different.

"We're snowed in!" shouted Jane Jones,
and Lucy shouted back, "So are we!"

Mr Billings had already been out quite early and dug and dug, so there was a path through the snow, leading around the side of the house, and a little way down the front drive, and slowly, slowly the path grew and they got a bit nearer to the front gate. They hadn't been going for very long before they heard voices from the house next door, and the sound of more shovels shovelling the snow, so Mr Billings shouted out over the fence, "Hello there!" and a voice shouted, "Hello there!" back, and suddenly Jane Jones appeared, high over the top of the fence, because she was being lifted up by Mr Jones.

"We're snowed in!" shouted Jane Jones, and Lucy shouted back, "So are we!" Then they all went back to work. It took a long time, and Lucy's hands got cold and her gloves got wet and her back ached, so after a while, she stopped trying to shovel the snow, and just watched the others, and looked around. Once or twice she went back into the house to listen, in case Rosie the baby had woken up. And Jessie, the big black labrador dog, rushed up and down in the snow and bounded and bounced and snuffled with her nose and dug and dug and dug (but in all the wrong places, and not helpfully at all!) and had a wonderful time.

After a while, Rosie did wake up, so Lucy went inside with her mother to get her up. They dressed her in her red snowsuit and her wellington boots with the frogs on, and then they brought her outside and set her down on the snowy path. And she stared and stared and *stared*, and pointed and smiled, and looked at Lucy and then back again at the snow. And Lucy said, "Snow. That's snow, baby," and Mrs Billings said it, too. "Snow, Rosie – that's the snow."

But Rosie just went on looking and looking, and after a minute, she bent down very carefully and picked up some snow in her hand and smiled, and she liked it so much that she picked up some more. But this time, she put her hand up to her face and began to *eat* the snow, and then she didn't like it at all. She made a dreadful, frowny face, and tried to spit the snow out and then to throw it away, and when she couldn't, but just felt it all wet and melty on her hands, she started to cry. So they took her back inside, and Mrs Billings said that perhaps when they had finished clearing the path, and the Joneses had finished clearing theirs, so that they could get through, they would all like to come and have a hot drink in the kitchen of Beehive Cottage.

So Lucy went out and called over the fence and asked them and they said yes, please, they certainly would. The path through the snow had reached almost to the front gate by now, so Lucy went down it and pushed through the piles of snow for the last little way, and just managed to climb onto the gate.

But just beyond the gate, where the lane dipped down, the snow was so high it was like a hill. And Lucy could see, as far as she could *up* the lane, that it was deep, deep, and rounded on top, as if somebody had piled up a lot of white pillows and cushions.

Then she said, "How will we get out? Will you have to dig with the shovels all the way up to the High Street?" But Mr Billings said No, the council men would come with the snow plough and clear the snow away, because it was much too deep up the lane for them to move it, and almost certainly right as far as the main Griffield road, too.

And he told her about a snow plough and what it looked like, and how it could make a path through the deep snow in just a few minutes.

"When will it come, oh *when*?" Lucy asked, because she very much wanted to see it.

But Mr Billings said Ah, that was the trouble, it might not be for a few days, because there weren't very many snow ploughs to go round, and they had to clear all the main roads first. It would take them quite a long time to get down to all the little side lanes like theirs.

So Lucy looked hard for a long time at the snow, and suddenly she wasn't sure if she would like being cut off for a very long time, and not be able to get out into the lane or walk up to the village, and to Mrs Dobby's post office shop, or to the playgroup, when it started again.

But just as she was worrying about it all, she heard a shout, and there stood Mr Jones with his spade, and snow all around him, right beside the gate. After a few more minutes, Lucy's father and brother Ben shouted too, and they had got the path through the snow all the way down to the gate on their side, so that all the Joneses could come in, though the path was very narrow and very slippery, and they had to walk very carefully indeed. But Lucy's mother said that she was going to sprinkle a lot of salt on the path, and that would melt the hard, icy snow, and stop it being so slippery to walk on.

Then everybody sat around the big kitchen table at Beehive Cottage and warmed their cold fingers on mugs of hot soup and told stories about other winters when the snow had come to Codling

They warmed their cold fingers on mugs of hot soup.

Village. And suddenly, in the middle of it all, Rosie the baby said very loudly, "Snow!" Only she wrinkled up her nose and blew down it at the same time as she said it, so that the word came out sounding very funny indeed. But still, it was quite clear, it was the word *Snow*.

"She said 'snow'!" Lucy and Jane both shouted out together.

"Snow," said Rosie again. "Snow. Snow." And each time, she wrinkled up her nose and blew down it as she said it. Then they all cheered and clapped their hands, which made her very excited and pleased, so that she clapped back, and went on and on saying, "Snow." Which was really very clever, because apart from something that sounded a bit like "Mum, Mum" and something else that sounded a bit like "Ben, Ben", Rosie the baby hadn't said any words at all yet. *Snow* was her very first really proper word!

Then the Joneses said that they had better be getting back to the house next door, and Lucy Billings' father said that *he* had better get on with seeing how the poor old hens were in their orchardy bit at the bottom of the garden. He said he thought he could get down there all right, because the wind had made the snow drift at the front of the house more than at the back, though it was still very deep over the garden.

And just when they were leaving, Mrs Jones said that she remembered she hadn't got any onions, and could Lucy's mother possibly lend her one. And Mrs Billings said that she certainly could, because of having done the Really Big Shop the day before, and did the Joneses need anything else, and they said that they had almost run out of washing-up liquid. So Mrs Billings fetched them a bottle of that, too.

Then brother Ben said that perhaps as they had got so much of everything, they had better pin a notice onto the gate post saying what they had to lend to anyone who had run out of anything. Which they all said would have been a very good idea, except that nobody would be able to get through the snow to the bottom of the lane, to read it!

"Besides," said Lucy's mother, "the snow plough will get through soon and Mrs Dobby will open her shop."

But the snow plough did not get through to Codling Village for three whole days, and by that time, a lot of people had been out with spades and shovels and cleared a path through to Mrs Dobby's post office shop.

And the very first person to get through to the village from the outside was not the man

76

with the snow plough at all, it was Frank the milkman, going very slowly and carefully with his milk float, whiny-whiny-rattle-chink. He came slipping and sliding down the slope into the village at eleven o'clock on Thursday morning, and stopped outside the post office shop. But he couldn't manage to deliver the bottles of milk to every house, as usual, because of the snow, and so he took out all the crates and set them up on the path outside Mrs Dobby's shop. Then Mrs Dobby telephoned to two people, asking them to come and fetch their milk, and those two people telephoned another two people, until everybody in Codling Village knew that the milk had arrived. And when Mark-by-the-pond's mother telephoned to the Joneses at Old Leas Farmhouse, Jane Jones came down her own path and up the path of Beehive

Cottage, very carefully, and knocked on the back door, and told the Billingses about the milk.

So then Mr Billings went down to the shed and got out the old sledge, and put Lucy onto it, and he pulled her all the way up the lane and into the High Street, on the path that had been cleared through the snow.

Lots of other people were going up to collect their milk too, and they all called out to each other, and said what would they do without Frank the milkman, and altogether it was a very jolly, friendly morning indeed.

Mrs Dobby's post office shop was so full and so busy that she said she was going to run out of a lot of things very soon. But Lucy Billings said that it was all right, because they had plenty of everything, after having done the Really Big Shop, so they